THE FARMYARD JAMBOREE

For Richard Scholtz; I dance every time he plays! — M. R. M.
To my friend Serge — S. F.

Barefoot Books,
124 Walcot Street
Bath BA1 5BG, UK

Barefoot Books
2067 Massachusetts Ave
Cambridge, MA 02140, USA

Text copyright © 2005 by Margaret Read MacDonald
Illustrations copyright © 2005 by Sophie Fatus
The moral right of Margaret Read MacDonald to be identified as the author and Sophie Fatus
to be identified as the illustrator of this work has been asserted

First published in Great Britain by Barefoot Books, Ltd and in the United States of America by Barefoot Books, Inc in 2005
This paperback edition printed in 2006
First published as *A Hen, A Chick and A String Guitar*

This book was typeset in Bembo Schoolbook 29 on 37 point and Cerigo Bold 36 point
The illustrations were prepared in acrylics and pastels

Graphic design by Judy Linard, London
Reproduction by Bright Arts, Singapore
Printed and bound in China by Printplus Ltd.

This book has been printed on 100% acid-free paper

ISBN 1-84686-031-8

The Library of Congress cataloged the hardcover edition as follows:

MacDonald, Margaret Read, 1940-
  A hen, a chick, and a string guitar / retold by Margaret Read
MacDonald ; illustrated by Sophie Fatus.
      p. cm.
  Summary: A cumulative tale from Chile that begins with a hen and
ends with sixteen different animals and a guitar.
  ISBN 1-84148-796-1 (alk. paper)
  [1. Folklore—Chile.] I. Fatus, Sophie, ill. II. Title.

PZ8.1.M15924Iah 2005
398.2'0983'0452—dc22

2004017830

British Cataloguing-in-Publication Data: a catalogue record for
this book is available from the British Library

3 5 7 9 8 6 4

THE FARMYARD JAMBOREE

Inspired by a Chilean folktale

written by Margaret Read MacDonald

illustrated by Sophie Fatus

Barefoot Books
Celebrating Art and Story

Grandpa gave me a clucking red hen.

"Cluck! Cluck! Cluck! Cluck! Cluck!"

Ay! Ay! Ay! What a fine hen!
"Cluck! Cluck! Cluck! Cluck! Cluck!"
One day that hen
Gave me a chick.
I had a hen,
And I had a chick.

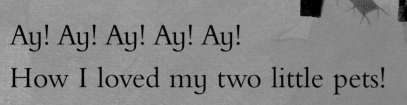

Ay! Ay! Ay! Ay! Ay!
How I loved my two little pets!

Grandma gave me a quacking white duck.

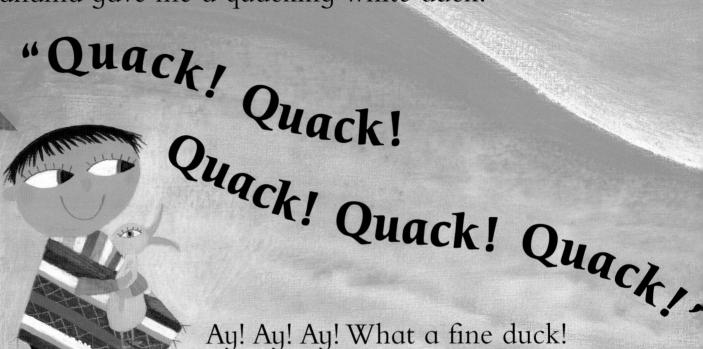

"**Quack! Quack!**
Quack! Quack! Quack!"

Ay! Ay! Ay! What a fine duck!
"Quack! Quack! Quack! Quack! Quack!"
One day that duck
Gave me a duckling.

I had a duck,
And I had a duckling.
I had a hen,
I had a chick.

Ay! Ay! Ay! Ay! Ay!
How I loved my four little pets!

Uncle gave me a purring yellow cat.

"Purr! Purr! Purr!"

Ay! Ay! Ay! What a fine cat!
"Purr! Purr! Purr!"
One day that cat
Gave me a kitten.

I had a cat,
And I had a kitten.
I had a duck.
I had a duckling.
I had a hen.
I had a chick.

Ay! Ay! Ay! Ay! Ay!
How I loved my six little pets!

Auntie gave me a barking black dog.

"Woof! Woof! Woof! Woof! Woof! Woof!"

Ay! Ay! Ay! What a fine dog!
"Woof! Woof! Woof! Woof! Woof!"

One day that dog
Gave me a puppy.

I had a dog,
And I had a puppy.
I had a cat.
I had a kitten.
I had a duck.
I had a duckling.
I had a hen.
I had a chick.

Ay! Ay! Ay! Ay! Ay!
How I loved my eight little pets!

Brother gave me a bleating white sheep.

"Baa! Baa! Baa!"

Ay! Ay! Ay! What a fine sheep!
"Baa! Baa! Baa!"

One day that sheep
Gave me a lamb.

I had a sheep,
And I had a lamb.
A dog…a puppy.
A cat…a kitten.
A duck…a duckling.
A hen…a chick.

Ay! Ay! Ay! Ay! Ay!
How I loved my
ten little pets!

Sister gave me an oinking pink pig.

"Oink! Oink! Oink! Oink! Oink!"

Ay! Ay! Ay! What a fine pig!
"Oink! Oink! Oink! Oink! Oink!"
One day that pig
Gave me a piglet.

I had a pig,
And I had a piglet.
A sheep…a lamb.
A dog…a puppy.
A cat…a kitten.
A duck…a duckling.
I had a hen.
I had a chick.

Ay! Ay! Ay! Ay! Ay!
How I loved my twelve little pets!

Mother gave me a mooing brown cow.

"Moo! Moo! Moo!"

Ay! Ay! Ay! What a fine cow!
"Moo! Moo! Moo!"
One day that cow
Gave me a calf.

I had a cow,
And I had a calf.
A pig…a piglet.
A sheep…a lamb.
A dog…a puppy.
A cat…a kitten.
A duck…a duckling.
A hen…a chick.

Ay! Ay! Ay! Ay! Ay!
How I loved my fourteen pets!

Father gave me a neighing grey horse.

"Neigh! Neigh! Neigh!"

Ay! Ay! Ay! What a fine horse!
"Neigh! Neigh! Neigh!"
One day that horse
Gave me a colt.

I had a horse,
And I had a colt.

A cow…a calf!

A pig…a piglet!

A sheep…a lamb!

A dog…a puppy!

A cat…a kitten!

A duck…a duckling!

I had a hen,
And I had a chick.

Ay! Ay! Ay! Ay! Ay!
How I loved my sixteen pets!

My friend gave me a little guitar!

"Plunk! Plunk!

Plunk! Plunk! Plunk!"

Ay! Ay! Ay! What a fine guitar!
"Plunk! Plunk! Plunk! Plunk! Plunk!"

And every time I played my guitar
My pets all came from near and far...

The horse danced
And the colt danced!

The cow danced
And the calf danced!

The pig danced
And the piglet danced!

The sheep danced
And the lamb danced!

The dog danced
And the puppy danced!

The cat danced
And the kitten danced!

The duck danced
And the duckling danced!

The hen danced
And the chick danced!

They all danced
And I danced too!